Learn to Draw

STRUCTURAL WONDERS

www.av2books.com

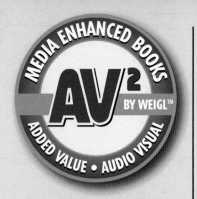

AV² provides enriched content that supplements and complements this book. Weigl's AV² books strive to create inspired learning and engage young minds in a total learning experience.

Your AV² Media Enhanced books come alive with...

Audio
Listen to sections of the book read aloud.

Key Words
Study vocabulary, and complete a matching word activity.

Go to **www.av2books.com**, and enter this book's unique code.

Video
Watch informative video clips.

Quizzes
Test your knowledge.

BOOK CODE

V 5 7 3 6 2 6

Embedded Weblinks
Gain additional information for research.

Slide Show
View images and captions, and prepare a presentation.

AV² by Weigl brings you media enhanced books that support active learning.

Try This!
Complete activities and hands-on experiments.

... and much, much more!

Published by AV² by Weigl
350 5th Avenue, 59th Floor
New York, NY 10118
Website: www.weigl.com   www.av2books.com

Library of Congress Cataloging-in-Publication Data

Structural wonders / edited by Heather Kissock.
    pages cm -- (Learn to draw)
ISBN 978-1-61913-243-6 (hardcover : alk. paper) -- ISBN 978-1-61913-248-1
(softcover : alk. paper)
1. Buildings in art--Juvenile literature. 2. Drawing--Technique--Juvenile
literature. I. Kissock, Heather.
NC825.B8S77 2012
743'.84--dc23
                            2012000467

Printed in the United States of America in North Mankato, Minnesota
1 2 3 4 5 6 7 8 9 0 16 15 14 13 12

042012
WEP050412

Senior Editor: Heather Kissock
Art Director: Terry Paulhus

Every reasonable effort has been made to trace ownership and to obtain permission to reprint copyright material. The publishers would be pleased to have any errors or omissions brought to their attention so that they may be corrected in subsequent printings.

Weigl acknowledges Getty Images as its primary image supplier for this title.

Contents

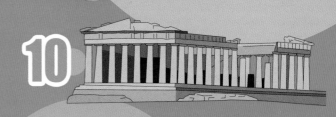

6

10

14

18

22

26

Why Draw?

Drawing is easier than you think. Look around you. The world is made of shapes and lines. By combining simple shapes and lines, anything can be drawn. An orange is just a circle with a few details added. A flower can be a circle with ovals drawn around it. An ice cream cone can be a triangle topped with a circle. Most anything, no matter how complicated, can be broken down into simple shapes.

circle

oval

circle

circle

triangle

Drawing helps people make sense of the world. It is a way to reduce an object to its simplest form, say our most personal feelings and thoughts, or show others objects from our **imagination**. Drawing an object can help you learn how it fits together and works.

What shapes do you see in this car?

It is fun to put the world onto a page, but it is also a good way to learn. Learning to draw even simple objects introduces the skills needed to fully express oneself visually. Drawing is an excellent form of **communication** and improves people's imagination.

Practice drawing your favorite structures in this book to learn the basic skills necessary to draw. You can use those skills to create your own drawings.

Structural Wonders

Drawing structures, such as buildings, bridges, and towers, is a great way to find out how they are constructed and how all their parts come together. As you draw the structures in this book, pay special attention to where certain parts have been placed and the role each part plays in creating the structure.

Planning and designing structures takes a long time. Every structure is built to serve a purpose. When designing a structure, **architects** must ensure that the structure is equipped with everything it needs to do the job required. They also have to make sure the structure is strong enough to withstand any challenges its location may bring, including weather and traffic.

Besides planning for the structure's practical needs, architects need to consider the appearance of the structure. How a structure looks sends a strong message to the people viewing it. Skyscrapers are often built to look strong and powerful. Many museums and art galleries have features that showcase creativity.

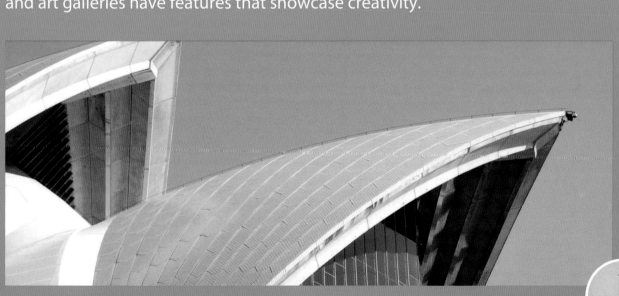

What are the Pyramids of Giza?

The Pyramids of Giza are **tombs** of three ancient Egyptian kings. They were built almost 4,500 years ago. There are three main pyramids at the site. The oldest and largest pyramid is called the Great Pyramid. It is one of the largest pyramids in the world. The other two pyramids are called the Pyramid of Khafre and the Pyramid of Menkaure. They were named after the kings for whom they were built.

The pyramids are located near Cairo, Egypt. They sit on the raised land of the Giza **Plateau**. The plateau is made of solid stone. It is able to support the weight of the pyramids.

Capstone
The capstone is a triangle-shaped stone that sits on top of a pyramid. It forms the pyramid's point. Capstones were usually made of stone but were often covered with gold. This made them shine brightly in the Sun.

Cornerstones
The cornerstones of the pyramids have balls and sockets built into them. This means that the stones are rounded and fit inside another stone. Ball and socket joints help the pyramid manage the **expansion** and **contraction** movements caused by heat and cold.

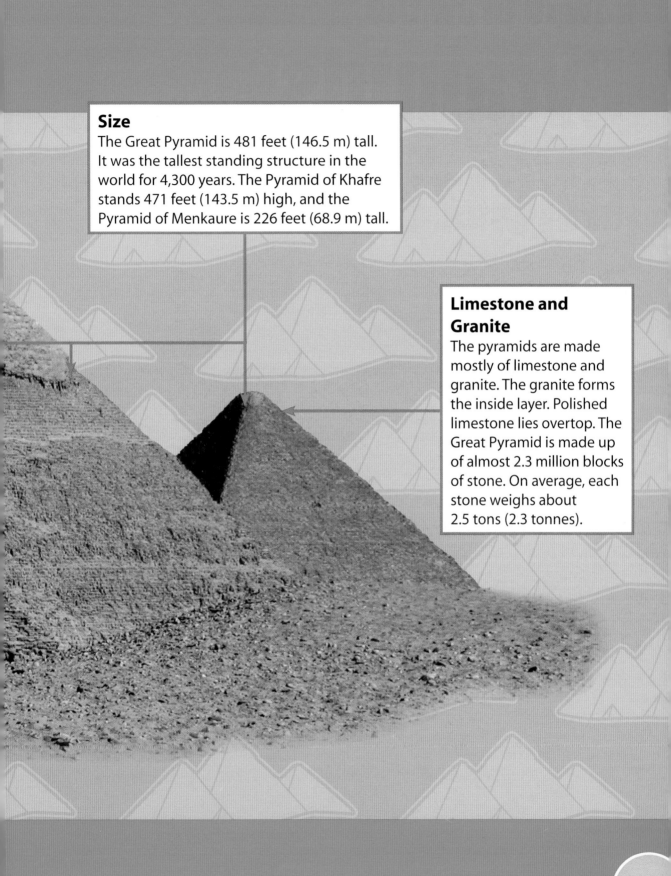

Size

The Great Pyramid is 481 feet (146.5 m) tall. It was the tallest standing structure in the world for 4,300 years. The Pyramid of Khafre stands 471 feet (143.5 m) high, and the Pyramid of Menkaure is 226 feet (68.9 m) tall.

Limestone and Granite

The pyramids are made mostly of limestone and granite. The granite forms the inside layer. Polished limestone lies overtop. The Great Pyramid is made up of almost 2.3 million blocks of stone. On average, each stone weighs about 2.5 tons (2.3 tonnes).

How to Draw the Pyramids of Giza

1 Draw a stick figure frame of the pyramids using three triangles.

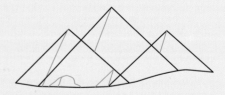

2 Draw the front edges of the pyramids, as shown.

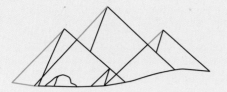

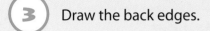

3 Draw the back edges.

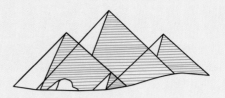

4 Now, add details to the pyramids.

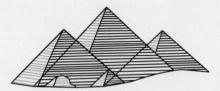

5 Draw the details on the back side.

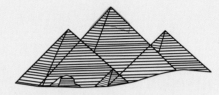

6 In this step, draw the limestone at the top of the pyramid.

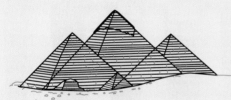

7 Draw the brick details and the small stones around the pyramids.

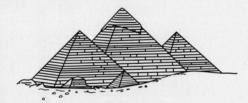

8 Erase the extra lines.

9 Color the image.

What is the Parthenon?

The Parthenon is a rectangular building with tall, white columns. It sits on top of a rocky hill in Athens, Greece. The building once served as a temple. It honored a goddess called Athena.

The Parthenon is made from a type of rock called marble. Marble is a soft rock. This means that people can carve it into different shapes. The Parthenon has many statues that have been crafted from marble.

Metopes
A series of marble panels run along the outside of the Parthenon's walls. These panels are called metopes. Each metope has a sculpture carved into it.

Porch
A eight-column porch sits at each end of the Parthenon. The porches support triangular areas called pediments. Each pediment features a **sculpture** that tells a story about ancient Greece.

Platform
The Parthenon was built on a platform. This platform is made up of three steps. The top step of the platform forms the floor of the building.

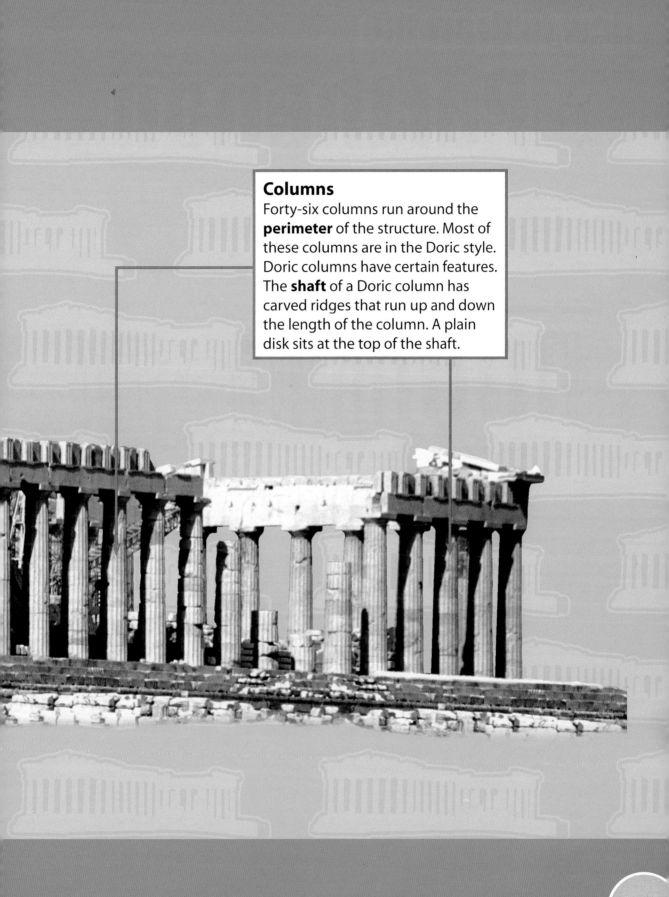

Columns

Forty-six columns run around the **perimeter** of the structure. Most of these columns are in the Doric style. Doric columns have certain features. The **shaft** of a Doric column has carved ridges that run up and down the length of the column. A plain disk sits at the top of the shaft.

How to Draw the Parthenon

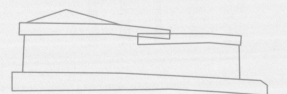

1 Draw a stick figure frame of the Parthenon using straight lines.

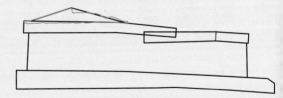

2 Now, draw the pediment.

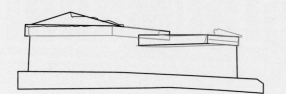

3 Next, draw the outline of the metope panels, as shown.

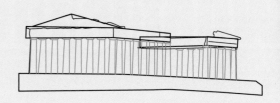

4 In this step, draw the columns.

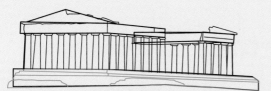

5 Draw the platform.

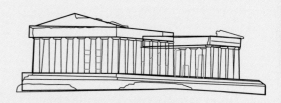

6 Add details to the columns.

7 Draw details on the metope panels and platform.

8 Erase the extra lines.

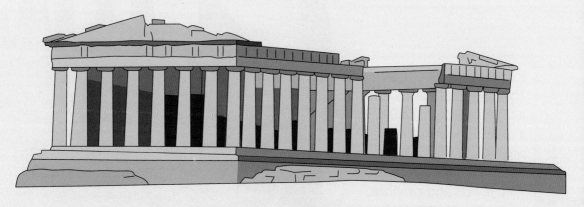

9 Color the image.

What is the Taj Mahal?

The Taj Mahal is located in Agra, India. It is a mausoleum. This is a type of building that is used as a **monument** to honor someone. It usually has the tomb of that person inside it.

The Taj Mahal was built because of a great love. An emperor built the Taj Mahal as a monument to his beloved wife. The words Taj Mahal mean "Crown Palace."

Minarets
Four minarets, or towers, make up the four corners of the Taj Mahal. Each of the four minarets has three balconies. They are connected by a winding stairway. Like the main dome, each minaret is capped with a lotus flower pattern.

Plinth
The Taj Mahal stands on a raised platform called a plinth. The plinth looks pure white from a distance, but it is actually decorated with jewels and carvings.

Dome
The Taj Mahal's main dome sits above the center of the building. It rises more than 200 feet (61 m) in the air. The top of the dome is decorated with a lotus flower pattern. The lotus flower represents good fortune.

Iwan
Each side of the Taj Mahal features a large, arched porch called an iwan. Beside each iwan are two levels of similar, but smaller, iwans. The large iwans are decorated with gems and colored stones.

How to Draw the
Taj Mahal

  1 First, draw a stick figure frame of the Taj Mahal using straight lines.

2 Now, draw the domes, as shown.

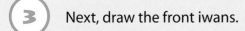

3 Next, draw the front iwans.

4 In this step, draw the minarets and plinth.

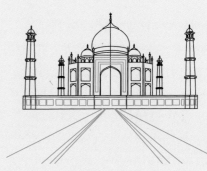

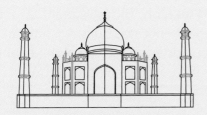

5 Add details to the domes and minarets.

6 Draw the front porch, and add details to the plinth and entry arch.

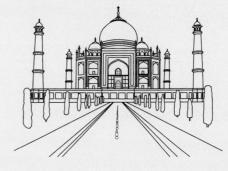

7 Draw the water fountains and trees on the porch, and add details to the iwans.

8 Erase the extra lines.

9 Color the image.

What is the Eiffel Tower?

Stretching high above Paris, France, the Eiffel Tower stands as a symbol of the city. The tower was built in the late 1880s by a French **engineer** named Gustave Eiffel. It was created for a large fair that featured displays from around the world.

The Eiffel Tower is made mainly of iron. When it was first built, many people thought it looked strange. Some believed it destroyed the beauty of the city. Today, it is difficult to imagine Paris without its tower.

Height

Today, the Eiffel Tower stands 1,063 feet (324 m) high. This is 39 feet (12 m) higher than when it was built. An antenna has been added to the top of the tower. This has increased its height.

Girders

Four columns of metal **girders** form the tower's triangular shape. The columns are set wide apart at the base of the structure. As they gain height, they curve inward before joining at the top.

Arches

Four giant arches sweep across the base of the tower, connecting the legs together. The arches provide support to the upper parts of the tower. They help transfer the weight from the top of the tower to the four metal columns at the base.

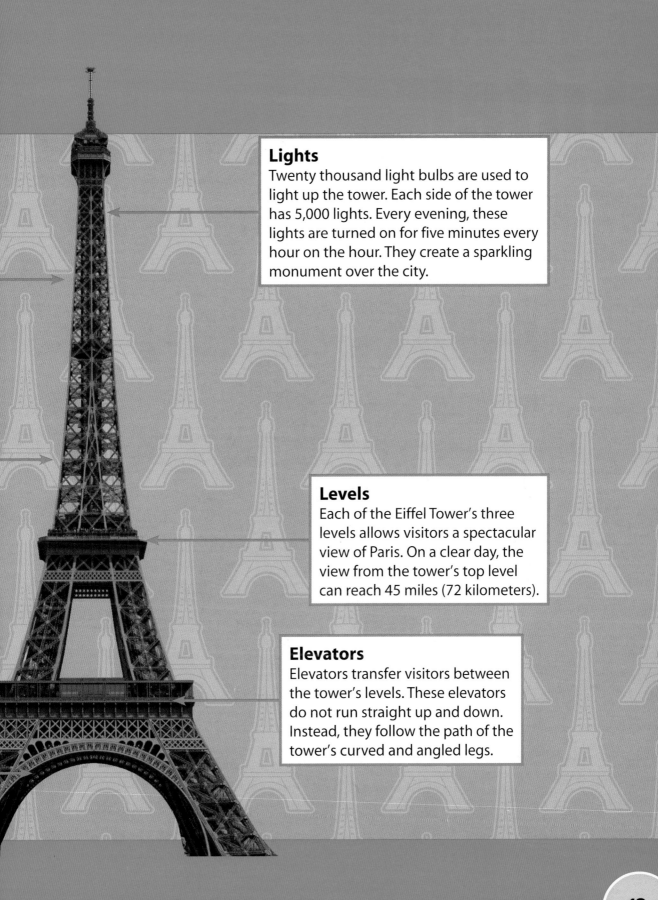

Lights

Twenty thousand light bulbs are used to light up the tower. Each side of the tower has 5,000 lights. Every evening, these lights are turned on for five minutes every hour on the hour. They create a sparkling monument over the city.

Levels

Each of the Eiffel Tower's three levels allows visitors a spectacular view of Paris. On a clear day, the view from the tower's top level can reach 45 miles (72 kilometers).

Elevators

Elevators transfer visitors between the tower's levels. These elevators do not run straight up and down. Instead, they follow the path of the tower's curved and angled legs.

How to Draw the Eiffel Tower

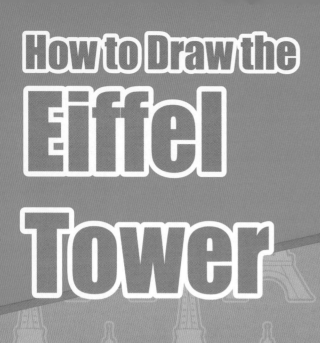

1 Draw a stick figure of the Eiffel Tower with straight lines, as shown.

2 Now, draw the girders and the platforms on the first and second levels.

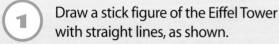

3 Next, draw the grids on the girders and platform on the third level.

4 In this step, draw the arches.

5 Draw the platforms on the first and second level.

6 Draw the top platform, as shown.

7 Next, draw the arches.

8 Erase the extra lines.

9 Color the image.

What is the Golden Gate Bridge?

The Golden Gate Bridge spans the mouth of San Francisco Bay. It is one of the United States' best-known landmarks. The bridge was built in the 1930s to connect Marin County to the city of San Francisco.

When it opened in 1937, the Golden Gate Bridge was the longest **suspension bridge** in the world. That record stood for 27 years. Today, the bridge is known for its tall towers, sweeping cables, and colorful orange frame.

Towers
The bridge's towers stretch 746 feet (227 m) above the water. They help support the weight of the roadway.

Roadway
The roadway of the Golden Gate Bridge hangs from cables. These cables extend across the bridge's entire span. They run through the bridge's two towers.

Cables

The bridge's main support cables are attached to **anchorages** that are built into the ground on both sides of the bridge. These cables help keep the tower firmly in place.

Size

The bridge is 8,981 feet (2,737 m) long. It weighs 887,000 tons (804,673 tonnes).

Paint

The Golden Gate Bridge's orange paint provides a splash of color. It takes 38 painters, working year-round, to maintain the paint on the bridge.

How to Draw the
Golden Gate Bridge

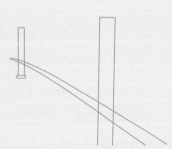

1 Draw a stick figure of the Golden Gate Bridge with straight lines, as shown.

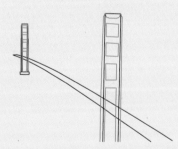

2 Draw the towers.

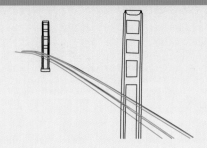

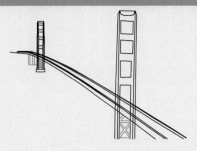

3 Now, draw the roadway.

4 Next, draw the foundation and base of the towers.

5 In this step, draw the main cables.

6 Draw the ocean and land, as shown.

7 Draw the supporting cables.

8 Erase the extra lines.

9 Color the image.

What is the Sydney Opera House?

Facing toward one of the most well-known harbors in the world, the Sydney Opera House greets people from land, sea, and air. The Sydney Opera House is a world-class performing arts center. People come to Australia from all over the world to see operas and ballets being performed here.

Due to its unique design, the Sydney Opera House is also one of Australia's major tourist attractions. More than 200,000 people take a guided tour of the building every year.

Shells
The Sydney Opera House has three sections of vaulted shells. The tallest group of shells houses a concert hall. The center shells house a theater. The smallest shells contain a restaurant.

Podium
The shells sit on top of a vast, stepped platform. This platform is called the podium.

Roof Tiles
The glossy white roof tiles of the Sydney Opera House reflect the sky. The roof is decorated with more than one million tiles.

Height
The top peak of the Sydney Opera House is 220 feet (67 m) high.

How to Draw the
Sydney Opera House

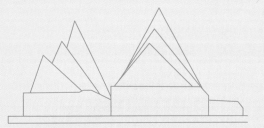

1 Draw a stick figure frame of the Sydney Opera House using triangles and straight lines.

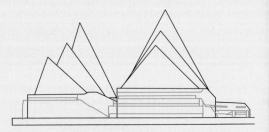

2 Draw the podium.

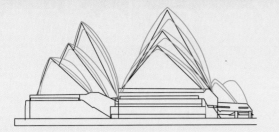

3 Next, draw the shells.

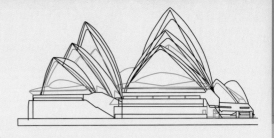

4 Draw the details inside the shells.

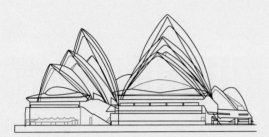

5 Add details to the podium.

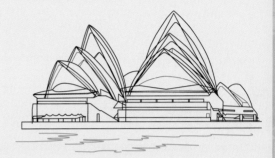

6 Next, draw the sea.

7 Draw small lines on the shells and podium, as shown.

8 Erase the extra lines.

9 Color the image.

Test Your Knowledge of Structural Wonders

1. What is a capstone?

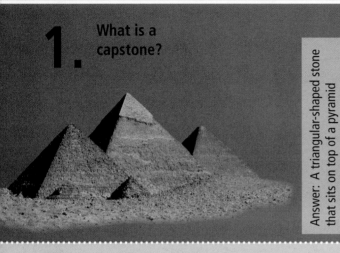

Answer: A triangular-shaped stone that sits on top of a pyramid

2. Who was the Parthenon built to honor?

Answer: The goddess Athena

3. What does Taj Mahal mean?

Answer: Crown Palace

4. How many light bulbs does it take to light up the Eiffel Tower?

Answer: 20,000

5. What type of bridge is the Golden Gate Bridge?

Answer: Suspension bridge

6. What is the Sydney Opera House's main feature?

Answer: The white shells that form its roof

Want to learn more? Log on to av2books.com to access more content.

30

Draw an Environment

Materials
- Large white poster board
- Internet connection or library
- Pencils and crayons or markers
- Glue or tape

Steps
1. Complete one of the structure drawings in this book. Cut out the drawing.
2. Use this book, the internet, and a library to find out about your structure and the environment around it.
3. Think about the features of this environment. What does it look like? What sorts of plants or other objects are found near it? Is there water? Are there other buildings or structures in its environment? What kinds of structures are these? What other important features might you find in this structure's environment?
4. On the large white poster board, draw an environment for your structure. Be sure to place all the features you noted in step 3.
5. Place the cutout structure in its environment with glue or tape. Color the structure's environment to complete the activity.

Glossary

anchorages: structures that supply a secure hold for something else

architects: people who design buildings

communication: the sending and receiving of information

contraction: the act of shrinking

engineer: someone who applies scientific principles to the design of structures

expansion: the act of widening

girders: beams used to support a structure

imagination: the ability to form new creative ideas or images

monument: a structure constructed as a memorial

perimeter: the outer limits of an area

plateau: flat and table-like land, usually higher than the land around it

sculpture: a work of art crafted from clay, rock, or metal

shaft: the principle section of a column

suspension bridge: a bridge that has the roadway suspended from cables

tombs: burial places

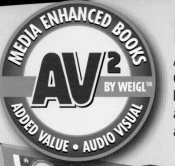

Log on to www.av2books.com

AV[2] by Weigl brings you media enhanced books that support active learning. Go to www.av2books.com, and enter the special code found on page 2 of this book. You will gain access to enriched and enhanced content that supplements and complements this book. Content includes video, audio, weblinks, quizzes, a slide show, and activities.

Audio
Listen to sections of the book read aloud.

Video
Watch informative video clips.

Embedded Weblinks
Gain additional information for research.

Try This!
Complete activities and hands-on experiments.

WHAT'S ONLINE?

Try This!	Embedded Weblinks	Video	EXTRA FEATURES
Complete an interactive drawing tutorial for each of the six structural wonders in the book.	Learn more about each of the six structural wonders in the book.	Watch a video about structural wonders.	**Audio** Listen to sections of the book read aloud.
			Key Words Study vocabulary, and complete a matching word activity.
			Slide Show View images and captions, and prepare a presentation.
			Quizzes Test your knowledge.

AV[2] was built to bridge the gap between print and digital. We encourage you to tell us what you like and what you want to see in the future.

Sign up to be an AV[2] Ambassador at www.av2books.com/ambassador.